THis is A VERY SiLLY Book

By Lala

First published in India in 2016 by Harper Kids
An imprint of HarperCollins *Publishers*

Text and Illustrations © Khushnaz Lala 2016

P-ISBN: 978-93-5264-116-1
E-ISBN: 978-93-5264-117-8

2 4 6 8 10 9 7 5 3 1

HarperCollins *Publishers*

A-75, Sector 57, Noida, Uttar Pradesh 201301, India
1 London Bridge Street, London, SE1 9GF, United Kingdom
Hazelton Lanes, 55 Avenue Road, Suite 2900, Toronto, Ontario M5R 3L2
and 1995 Markham Road, Scarborough, Ontario M1B 5M8, Canada
25 Ryde Road, Pymble, Sydney, NSW 2073, Australia
195 Broadway, New York, NY 10007, USA

Printed and bound at Thomson Press (India) Ltd

THiS iS A VERY SiLLY Book

(For Agastya and Shanaya)

HARPER KIDS

This   is a very silly book.

That's because my
friends who live here
are
very
very
VERY

silly.

Don't say I didn't warn you...

_____ is a pirate.

His moustache is
drawn on,

but his chest hair
isn't.

This is my friend _____.

He is really, REALLY tall!

He never wears clothes.
Even when we go out to eat
in fancy places.

_____ had a
bad haircut.

Please don't stare at him,
it will make him

self-conscious.

This is an orange.

He doesn't look like
the other oranges,
but he knows that
his outsides don't
define him.

_____ just drank
the Milky Way.

She forgot that she's
lactose intolerant.

Maybe you should turn the page...

_____ is a
floating rag doll head.

It's a little creepy
but she's really nice
once you get to know her.

_____ likes to eat crayons.

When she grows up, she's going to be a philosophical genius who will change the world.

This is my heart.
It is my best friend.

I'm not sure why it
looks like that.

I should probably get
it checked.